Reign of Darkness

Gair McDonald

Contents

Dedication

To my family and friends, who have helped me through these strange times.

About the Author

Born in 1976, Aberdeen, Scotland, Gair Mcdonald is an ambitious writer. He is an enthusiastic and passionate screenwriter who has written several screenplays to date. He has a love of 'film' and cites Orson Welles, David Lean, Alfred Hitchcock, Wes Craven, Steven Spielberg, JJ Abrams and Christopher Nolan, to name but a few as the people he most admires.

His achievements to date worth noting are:

- British Short Screenplay Later Round 2004.
- The Next Generation Independent Film Festival 2017 WINNER "Best Creature Feature" - *The Gurel* (renamed Darkness Never Fades).
- An honourable mention from the prestigious Nicholls Screenwriting Competition in 2018, close to a Quarter-Finals placing with his war drama *'The Legend of Corporal Pike'*.

He is also credited as an Associate Producer on the acclaimed short film, *the Dancer & the Boy (2014).*

He has latterly ventured into writing (short) novels, his first one being '*Blackwood Manor*', which he has now followed up with *Reign of Darkness: The Adventures of Hans Reigns.*

Captivated with stories from a young age, he cites Stephen King, Jonathan Maberry, Brian Moreland and Richard Chizmar as the authors who inspired him to venture down this way.

Prologue

Hans Reigns was the last in line of the Reigns family. His family has its own folklore in his home country of Ubaria, a small country situated in deep darkest far Eastern Europe. The Reigns were a poor family who struggled to survive, in contrast to the neighbouring Valdes family who were steeped in power and wealth. Over the centuries, both families feuded over land which ended in bloodshed. However, its 'unnatural' repercussions continue to this day. Myth and legend have it that Hans was given up as a baby to the Ubarian Royal Family. In time, Hans learned to fend and fight for himself as the forces of darkness descended.

Hans Reigns never once considered himself as Royal Blood. The only thing he believed in was that it was his destiny to rid the world of evil to avenge the death of 'both his families'. He made that his lifetime vow. Living as a 'drifter' from his early teens, Hans travelled through his homeland encountering and battling with the 'supernatural beings'. It was Han's mission to wipe out the Valdes bloodline, which was engulfed in evil. Fortunately, with his efforts and determination, he was able to eradicate the Valdes bloodline once and for all. Consequently, he became well-known as a brave and fearless young boy in Urbaria. It didn't take long for some of Ubaria's small villages and people of importance to call upon the help of Hans Reigns. However, at the same time, the forces of evil vowed to destroy him.

Years passed, and Hans turned twenty-one. Soon after his twenty-first birthday, Hans sought out Father Dovak, the country's longest-serving priest at a rundown church. Father Dovak informed Hans of his 'birth' mother and her 'visions' of the Zvekios, Ubarian word for 'The Beast'. Father Dovak claimed that the Zvekios had made him 'eternal'.

Hans listened to Father Dovak, but he was sceptical about the authenticity of this claim. However, that night, when he slept, he was disturbed by some strange visions. They were the same visions his mother had of the Zvekios, as Father Dovak had described earlier that day. At dawn, Hans returned to the rundown church to confront Father Dovak. He was already enlightened that Hans would come looking for him. Hans was enraged; he produced a small silver crossbow from under his long overcoat and vowed to avenge the death of his adopted family. The shots from the crossbow had no effect on Father Dovak who 'tempted' Hans to 'follow' the Zvekios. Hans produced a capsule from his overcoat and threw it on the floor beside Dovak. The capsule emitted a smoke which ‘burned’ the side of Father Dovak’s face. This action was quite unexpected for Father Dovak, and it prompted him to retreat, with his parting words, ‘until next time’.

Chapter One

The country of Ubaria, even to this day, manages to attract the many with mystery and myth. And one such person was Diane Derry, who arrived in Gurikel, the capital of Ubaria, one mid-afternoon. Diane, in her mid-thirties, stuck out like a sore thumb wearing designer clothes, bag and travel case. Furthermore, being a bright redhead made her look like a beacon.

Diane looked up at the October sky, filled with grey clouds and dampness.

Just perfect: she thought. However, as she moved further, she was rather disappointed. This was not what she was used to, not at all. Diane dreamt of sandy beaches, blue skies and warm golden sunshine as she wandered the streets, which impoverished, dirty and desperate. Diane dragged her travel case up the streets which bounced awkwardly along the cobbles. At every third doorway, sat a beggar. Male, female, old, young - Diane couldn't possibly tell with them being wrapped up in rags protecting them from the October air. Diane, the total outsider, felt every stare as she walked past. Sellers from street stalls would 'dangle' their products in front of Diane, who smiled politely but showed no interest. She wanted a room, any room and now.

'Crack'. Diane's heel from her shoe snapped between the uneven street cobbles. She looked up the skies which were darkening by the minute.

Fortunately, Diane found the taxi easily. As it journeyed to her accommodation, it took Diane to steep and twisting roads. A mountainous region dominated the background. However, Diane was too focussed on her broken shoe and if it could be mended to care about the sights. She was least interested about where she was headed or if the tin can of the vehicle that she was in would get her there as it '*rattled*' nonstop and made an uncomfortable '*clicking*' noise over every bump.

After about thirty-five minutes, Diane arrived at her destination. The taxi driver squeezed his bulbous head out of the window, almost knocking off his flat cap. Diane paid the driver who responded in kindness with a 'grunt'.

Diane inspected the street, up and down; a few children chased a football, '*giggling*' and '*laughing*'. Before Diane could set foot in her hotel, a high pitched '*squeaking*' noise made her almost jump. It was impossible to say who was more scared, Diane or the rat that she just crossed paths with. Diane took a breath as she watched the rat, nearly the size of a small cat heading towards the group of children further up the street.

Diane looked up at the entrance to the hotel building. She attempted to make out the engraved writing above the doorway, which read 'Duvi Init'. It was a bed and breakfast which looked quite old from the outside. Diane walked in and was welcomed by the stench of musty air which hit the back of her throat that became stronger with every step she took. She screwed her face up in disgust.

Diane stood alone in a small cramped reception area; the decor resembled being stuck in a time warp, tasteless and ancient. A few photos of the former Ubarian Royal Family decorated the walls. Diane approached the desk and went to strike the reception bell with the palm of her hand. Before she could strike the bell, two unsavoury looking characters, large in size appeared from a back room. Both wore leather jackets. One of them held a handful of cash; the other flicked a cigarette away as he walked by Diane. She felt quite uneasy by this gesture. She wondered if she had made the right decision concerning the accommodation. Diane felt a bad vibe immediately. She was about to turn to leave when a voice boomed.

"What you want?" Asked a voice in broken English.

It was too late. Diane turned to be greeted by a huge, bald proprietor cleaning a large pint glass with a dish towel that had seen better days, but certainly not a washing machine. The proprietor wore a white apron decorated with stains and various colours.

"I'd like a room please." Diane spoke somewhat nervously. The proprietor eyed Diane up and down. "How many nights you want?"

"Seven... Seven nights." Diane said, swallowing a lump in her throat.

The proprietor turned to a board, which didn't even sit straight as it hung on the wall. From the six keys which hung from it, he grabbed a small key and slammed it on the table.

"Room three." Growled the proprietor, pointing his index finger in the direction of a set of stairs in the corner of the reception area. Diane slid the key off the table before pulling the travel case towards the corner stairs. Diane beamed a polite smile to the proprietor. "Thank you." The proprietor nodded his head in return.

Diane struggled to pull her travel case up the small set of twisty stairs, eventually reaching the first floor of the two-floor building. A glance on the left-hand side of the corridor showed room number two. Diane covered her mouth as she went further down the corridor. The stench was becoming more and more unbearable, hitting the back of her throat with a vengeance. Diane gave out a couple of coughs.

Room number three was hardly spacious. It contained one single bed, a desk and a mirror. '*Hardly the Ritz*', Diane thought. She looked out the window which overlooked the street below. It was dark and quiet. The only sound that could be heard was of the dogs that were chasing and barking at each other. Diane dared not check the condition of the bathroom, not yet anyway. Instead, she looked for an electrical power point. She found the sole socket in the corner. She took her laptop out from the bag and kept in on the bed. The wire from her laptop managed to stretch to the socket, just. As she turned the power switch on, the laptop fired up and revealed a screensaver photo of a handsome young man around Diane's age, dark-haired, bearded and happy. Diane was quite surprised seeing this picture. She had never set this as a screensaver. She touched the laptop screen, but before she could even strike a button, something dropped on to the laptop. It was a black dot which suddenly moved, and then another black dot landed and scurried off the table. Diane looked above her to see a small nest of spiders. Dozens of babies were scurrying in all directions with the mother, slightly smaller the size of a child's hand looking down at Diane.

Diane immediately took out a notebook from her bag and tried to kill these tiny creatures by striking the notebook against them. She could smash a few of them; the rest of the spiders, along with their mother, disappeared.

"God, I just can't work here." She muttered under her breath and shut the laptop lid.

Diane was very tried. She had been awake since morning and now just wanted to rest. Ignoring the spiders, she lay on the bed. As she closed her eyes and tried to sleep, a myriad of thoughts went through her mind from the day, the flight over, her broken shoe, the spiders sharing the room with her but most of all the handsome man on her laptop - *her* handsome man. Something was wrong about this place.

Before Diane could finally drift off to sleep, she heard a disturbance out in the street. Her eyes became wide, alert. She could hear foreign voices become louder and louder. It seemed like an altercation. She focused her attention on the voices in an attempt to grasp what this argument was all about. Suddenly Diane heard the loud '*smash'* of glass. Her eyes now became even wider in fear. This was too close for comfort.

Diane's curiosity got the better of her; one of her habits, and a bad one at that, the habit of nosiness. It came with the territory. She tiptoed, barefooted to the window and peered out between the joints in the curtain. The dimly lit street revealed two figures on the ground, motionless. Another figure stood over them. Diane made out that the standing figure wore a long coat which moved like a cape in a breeze. The figure, like a sixth sense, turned and looked up in the direction of Diane's window. Diane immediate pulled the curtains together tightly. Panic etched over her face as she took a couple of breaths.

Chapter Two

The following morning when Diane woke up, she recalled everything that happened last night. She didn't know how she had fallen asleep, but she was relaxed that the night had passed. Lying on her bed, she looked up at the corner of the room and the after-effects of the previous night battle with the eight-legged army that had occupied the room. Dots were smeared in the roof, which was the combination of squashed spiders and the stains of blood and guts. But where was the mother? The 'monster' that ruled the room by fear.

She got out of bed and shuffled the table and chair for any clues of the monster's whereabouts. This battle was for another day, or maybe never?

Diane approached the proprietor at the reception area; the proprietor wore the same stained apron from the day before as he wrote in a notebook. The proprietor caught Diane's stare but continued writing as if on purpose to annoy these 'foreigners'. Diane forced a '*cough*'.

"Excuse me?" The proprietor turned a beady eye in the direction of Diane. How dare she interrupt him whilst he was in full flow? The proprietor wrote a few more words before he gave Diane any attention.

"Yes."

“Do you have any glue?” Asked Diane.

The proprietor looked at Diane as if she had just arrived from the planet Mars, “What?”

“You know, glue?” Diane lifted up her broken shoe.

The proprietor gave out a murmur and then a grunt, “Give to me.”

Diane thought for a moment. Could she trust this stranger guy, with her shoe from the pair that cost over five hundred pounds? Nevertheless, she had no option other than trusting him. She reluctantly handed the shoe to the proprietor who immediately went away with it. Diane was fearful of the state the shoe would be returned in.

***

Light rain fell on the city of Gurikel. Diane held a map in her hand as she walked to the very spot the disturbance took place the previous night. There were no signs of anyone hanging around; the only evidence of any altercation was small patches of blood on the ground. ‘*A drunken altercation*’ Diane thought. Just like the ‘mysterious’ figure the night before. Diane turned her head towards her window.

Diane was barely a hundred yards up the road. She was too busy, with her head buried in a tourist map, to have an interest in a scooter that sped past her, jet black in colour. She flinched, pulling her bag strap over her shoulder. Thinking nothing of it, Diane continued her journey, oblivious to the scooter coming back around from behind her for a second pass. The engine roared close to her, causing Diane alarm. She turned her head. The figure on the scooter, with their face covered by the helmet, had seen her bag as too good an opportunity to miss. The scooter came to a stop, the figure lunged out and attempted to grab Diane's bag with one arm. Though Diane was scared to death, she stood her ground, dropping the map in the process. She glimpsed two passers-by and one elderly man peering from a doorway, all watching as if mugging was some regular sport. Maybe it was. However, the area seemed a popular hot spot for an ambush.

The scooter rider dismounted their vehicle playing 'tug-of-war' for Diane's handbag. Diane held her own, albeit briefly. The scooter rider finally overpowered Diane taking the handbag from her. Diane wasn't giving up without a fight.

"Oh no, you don't!" Diane cried out. She went for the scooter rider before they jumped back on their vehicle; however, she received a vicious kick to the stomach for her valiant efforts. Diane landed on the ground with a hard thump, hitting the side of her head in the process. She watched, in a dazed state as the scooter sped off into the distance. Turning her head, she watched the elderly man go back into the doorway. The show was over.

Diane clutched her head as she took a seat on the kerb. She fumbled in a jacket pocket and pulled out a crumpled Kleenex. She dabbed it on her head; the Kleenex was soon crimson with blood. Diane sat alone looking above at the darkening skies, rolling in wondering what the hell else could go wrong. Yet the situation didn't deter her, nor did the bang or graze to the head.

Still holding the Kleenex to the side of her head, Diane passed a stray ginger cat which *hissed* aggressively at her as she entered a small cafe. Diane snarled back, "same to you kitty!"

She took a seat in a corner and wondered if the population of strays matched the population of people. The three patrons in the cafe turned their head. Ina, the female cafe owner, in her fifties, spindly with hair resembling a bird's nest noticed all was not well and placed a glass of water in front of Diane.

"Thank you," said Diane. "Where am I… I mean what's the name of this place?"

Ina smiled, which masked the fact she couldn't speak a word of English.

Diane watched Ina retreat back to the counter area and sat and listened to the rhythmic, yet soothing pattern of the rain as it began to bounce off the cafe window. She picked up the menu sitting in front of her, not understanding one word; she looked to the heavens before putting the menu down. At that point, unbeknown to Diane, the cafe door slowly swung open with a *'creek'*. The cafe owner looked on in amazement, hands on her face. She began to mutter in her native language, which became louder and louder with excitement. Diane looked towards the counter area; a figure wearing a long overcoat and hat stood with their back to her. In their one hand was *her* handbag which, for Diane, was enough to light the blue torch paper.

"The son-of-a…" Diane said to herself before leaping up from her seat, dropping the blood-stained Kleenex to the ground. She meant business and certainly didn't care one bit about breaking up any cosy conversation. Diane approached the figure and attempted to snatch *her* handbag back. It wouldn't budge.

"Let go, thief!" Yelled Diane, much to the dismay of the cafe owner. "What's the matter? Have a guilty conscious?" Added Diane.

The figure turned and looked at Diane. He was a male, in his late forties with brown, grizzled hair; a small scar dominated on his forehead. This was Hans Reigns.

"I can report you to my embassy for this! Do you know that? They will lock you away!" Diane screamed.

Hans released his hold on the handbag which took Diane by surprise as contents spilt on the floor. Diane bent down to retrieve them.

"My apologies," smiled Hans, speaking in broken English, "But you did say let go." Diane ignored the sarcastic remark as she placed her belongings back in her handbag. Hans crouched down to face Diane. "For one, I am no thief, yes? And for another, I was returning your bag."

Hans picked up a card from the floor which read 'Diane Derry-Reporter'. Diane snatched the card back from Hans. "Give me that. That's a good excuse by the way."

"So, you are a reporter?" Asked Hans.

"Don't change the subject, you know I can *report* you." Snapped Diane.

Hans seemed unfazed. "Be my guest, and tell me Mrs Derry, did the person on the scooter dress like this?" Hans gestured to himself with both hands.

Diane was lost for words. Hans had her there. The great roving reporter, Diane Derry, was finally lost for words; courtesy of a man she met only a matter of moments ago.

Diane looked at Hans, sheepish. "And it's Miss…"

Hans 'tipped' his hat and bid the cafe owner good day before leaving.

Hans began to walk up the street before stopping to take a drink from a silver hipflask. Diane watched in the background, she was slightly irate, or in her words, "pissed off'. No one got the better of *this* reporter, let alone have the last word. Still, there was something about this guy, an air of intrigue surrounded her and Diane Derry was captivated to find out more.

Diane flinched, having flashbacks at every motor vehicle that screamed past; she kept an extra hold of her handbag for good measure. She wondered if this country had even heard of speed limits. *Most probably not*: she thought. Diane glimpsed Hans as he continued his walk up the street ahead, passing a cluster of rag covered civilians seated on the dust-layered pavement playing a game. Diane purposely moved onto the street area, out of any harm's way from the group of civilians. At a closer inspection, Diane saw that they were playing a game using sticks and stones, pushing the stones every so often, whatever that game maybe. All eyes turned to Diane as she passed the group; however, Diane's focus was on Hans as he turned down a side street.

Diane stopped at the top of the side street to see through a faint haze of nothing but bags of litter and scattered rubbish, the ideal breeding ground for rats. "So, you're Houdini now are you?"

Darkness had set, and back at the cafe, all was quiet and empty. The female cafe owner wiped down the tables, winding down for the day; she whistled a happy tune signing in her native language to faint music through the static that could be heard playing on a radio behind the counter. Out of nowhere, the cafe door swung open with a thunderous *crash* which shattered the glass panel. The music from the radio was replaced by very loud piercing static. The cafe owner took a few nervous steps back. She couldn't see anyone at the doorway but didn't count for the large dark-robed, hooded figure that stood over seven-feet tall, and loomed behind her until she walked backwards into it. She turned around; her eyes bulged wide in terror, she was face to face with hell itself – the Zvekios.

The cafe owner screamed out in horror before being overcome and paralysed with fear. She slumped to the ground, seemingly resigned to her fate. Tears ran down her thin, pale face.

"He was here, you had the opportunity and yet again you failed to take it," a deep, sinister and commanding voice echoed through the cafe like thunder. "Why?"

The cafe owner didn't answer; she couldn't answer.

"I asked why?" The figure demanded an immediate response. The cafe owner felt her heart racing as if it wanted to escape her rib cage. The woman broke out in a cold sweat. The figure asked the question once more, this time in the native language. The cafe owner closed her eyes and lowered her head. A bluish-grey skeletal hand with large fingers and elongated dark grey fingernails placed itself on top of the cafe owner's brunette wiry hair. The large fingers clamped itself across the cafe owner's head. There was no escape. Blood began to ooze through hair from the cafe owner's cranium as fingernails embedded into her skull like clamps. She looked up, mouth wide open; face all but void of life, a blank and hopeless expression. A sickening and gruesome *snapping* sound followed. The hand lifted the cafe owner's head, now detached from her spine; her headless body rolled harmlessly to the floor.

Chapter Three

On the outskirts of Gurikel stood a large cathedral, '*The Zainitial,*' which in Ubarian meant 'The Grand One.' Some claimed The Zainitial to be well over a thousand years old, others suggested it had stood since the beginning of time itself, whilst the 'crazies' out there believed it to be a portal between the Earth and an alien world. Everyone had their thoughts and beliefs of the cathedral.

Inside the grand cathedral, Diane sat on a pew at the front. The cathedral was busy with people observing, gazing in awe at the splendour of the architecture and the gold joints on the roof that ran down giant pillars. The roof was engraved with beautiful sculptures of Angels playing the trumpets. Diane looked at the beauty of the statue of Christ on the cross made entirely of marble. Despite making visitors awestruck, the cathedral was cold and draughty. Damp patches decorated parts of the roof and were in need of renovating.

Diane fumbled in her handbag for a folder, not taking her eyes of the statue of Christ. The pew *creaked* as someone took a seat beside Diane. Father Nosro Sellew, a large man, in his sixties, with thick grey hair and overgrown beard, looked at Diane who was busy sketching a drawing of the statue of Christ; he noticed her folder and paperwork sitting on the pew. "Beautiful, isn't it?" Said Father Sellew. Diane looked up and acknowledged Father Sellew with a polite smile.

"Did you know, that the statue of our Lord took over ten years to craft?" Father Sellew said.

"Well, I would say that was ten years well spent." Replied Diane.

"Indeed." Father Sellew nodded.

Father Sellew watched Diane collate her folder and paperwork, "Do you know the most amazing part of it all?"

"What might that be?" Inquired Diane.

"No one knew who produced this fine work of art." Father Sellew claimed.

Diane looked at Father Sellew, puzzled. "No one?"

"Some centuries ago or depending on what you believe, it was just there. It appeared like magic."

"Like magic?"

"Incredible, isn't it?"

Diane wasn't buying that story. Not one bit.

"I will tell you what's incredible. Someone crafted a beautiful fifty-foot tall work of art which was left as a centre piece here, and no one through the ages can report or witness anyone leaving this as a gift?" said Diane.

"Most peculiar indeed." Agreed Father Sellew.

Diane placed her folder in her bag, shook her head and frowned unsure what to make of Father Sellew's story or Father Sellew himself. For all, she knew Father Sellew could be a daft, crazy old man prone to the exaggeration of storytelling. "In that case then you have a centuries old mystery on your hands?" Diane claimed. Father Sellew forced a laugh which became too forceful, not to mention blatantly obvious, and created attention to the people in the cathedral. Diane rose to her feet; Father Sellew followed suit. He looked at Diane momentarily.

"Are you here on business or for pleasure?" Asked Father Sellew.

"Both." Replied Diane.

Diane began to shuffle out from the pew. Father Sellew wasn't letting her go that easily. "What is your line of work?" He asked.

"I am a writer, of sorts." Replied Diane.

"Of sorts? Interesting!" Quizzed Father Sellew.

That was it; Diane was giving him no more. No more crumbs or clues. Father Sellew frowned, almost in suspicion as he watched Diane leave.

Diane returned to her bed and breakfast accommodation before nightfall. She walked much to her pleasant surprise along the corridor without having to screw up her face from the foul stench that lingered. Diane entered room number three to discover her bed had been made with fresh bed sheets. She looked up to see no trace of any spiders; the evidence was cleaned up. Her room had been completely cleaned. Diane turned to her laptop on the desk to see her shoe sitting on top of it. She inspected the shoe. It was as good as new with no mark or scratches of any kind. Diane was dumbfounded. *How the hell did he manage that?* She thought.

Diane approached the reception desk, and before she could strike down on the bell, the proprietor appeared with a sparkling new apron and a name badge that read 'Mared'.

"So, you do have a name." Diane muttered.

Mared was quick to notice Diane's mended shoe in her hand, along with a sheet of paper.

"You like? You like?" Mared said excitedly.

"Yes. I have come to thank you. It's like new." Diane eyed Mared sceptically, wondering if this is the same guy that gave her practically one-word answers previously.

Mared gestured to Diane to wait a minute. Diane stood curious. He disappeared into a small room behind the reception. Diane wondered to herself what was coming here. Mared reappeared with his hands behind this back and with a mischievous smile on his face; he placed a glass jar on the reception desk. To Diane's horror, the jar contained the mother spider from her room, otherwise known as the 'monster'. She took a few nervous steps back. Diane couldn't even turn her head in the direction of the jar as she turned pale.

"I found this in your room, yes?" Mared said.

"No kidding," replied Diane.

Curiosity got the better of her; a quick turn of her head was enough to see the 'monster' in clear detail: jet black hair, thick hairy legs that reached out touching the top of the jar almost in slow motion, teasing which showed the grand scale of the 'monsters' size. A quick count showed three brownish-red spots on the back of the body and the eyes. A cluster of small, empty, dark and unforgiving eyes met Diane's stare. She felt hundreds of eyes staring back at her. Diane felt uneasy and swallowed nervously. The 'monster' wriggled and jumped around in the jar with such force that the jar slid closer to the edge of the table much to Mared's amusement as he pointed to the jar. Diane took a few more steps back, not finding anything funny whatsoever.

"You are going to kill it, aren't you? Or at least release it far away from here?" Diane asked puzzled. Mared picked up the jar, laughing. "No, no. I keep him or her." Diane looked in disbelief as Mared inspected the jar looking for some clue of the spider's sex. "I can't tell if it's a boy or girl?" Diane shook her head in total bewilderment.

"Tell me, why would you want to keep... *that*?" Diane inquired.

"I can keep as pet."

"A pet?" Diane looked at Mared.

Is this guy serious? She thought. "You can hardly give it a cuddle or take it out for walks?"

"No, but it will keep the mice and rats away, yes?" Asked Mared, knowing full well the 'monster' will.

Diane said, "Never mind the mice and rats, which by the way really isn't a great selling point; it will keep me away for one."

"I will put it away." Conceded Mared.

"I say that's a good idea." Agreed Diane in a sarcastic tone, however, with huge relief.

Mared picked up the jar, "I will take it outside, to my store shed."

"Your store shed? I take it that is where your mice and rat problem is?" Diane asked.

Mared ignored Diane's words as he walked away towards the back area, tapping on the glass jar which irritated the 'monster' at the same time.

Diane called out, “Well I hope your store shed is like a million miles from here.”

“You don’t have to worry. It will be fine, you will see.” Mared’s attempt to reassure Diane wasn’t convincing.

“I meant to ask. The name above your door, what does it mean?” Asked Diane.

“Duvi Init? That means ‘small place’.” Said Mared.

“Well with six rooms, that explains a lot.” Smiled Diane as a burst of laughter exploded from Mared, thinking it was the funniest joke he had ever heard.

“Very good! Very good!” Mared said applauding.

Diane rolled her eyes. *You guys around here are easily amused:* Diane thought. She quickly changed the subject.

“I must say you have cleaned the place well.” Diane said, looking around.

“I am happy! I won my money back. And a lot of it.” explained Mared. “I can afford some luxuries now.” This was a new man; a man that was on a roll and he was going to enjoy every minute of it.

“Like a new apron perhaps?” Asked Diane.

Mared smiled and nodded his head as he returned to the reception area. That explained the two characters Diane had seen on her arrival, leaving with a wad of cash.

"So, where you going today?" Inquired Mared.

Diane briefly looked at a sheet of paper in her hand, which was a phone bill, then at the photos of the Royal Family on the walls. It struck her.

"What about the Palace, is it far?" Asked Diane. Mared lowered his head, solemn.

Diane hoped she hadn't offended Mared in any way.

"You have to excuse me. The Royal Family proved a dark time in our country's history; not many visit there now." Mared shuffled away. However, he stopped and turned to face Diane.

"Why are you here?" Mared asked.

Diane swallowed before taking her time in giving an answer. "I am doing a project."

"A project?" Mared raised his eyebrow.

"Yes. On this country." Answered Diane.

Mared gave Diane a blank look, not showing any enthusiasm for Diane's project before mumbling a faint "good luck" and walking away with the jar containing the captured 'monster'.

***

It was around mid-day when Diane arrived at the Royal Palace, which in truth was nothing but an ancient crumbling ruin. Diane couldn't understand or believe all the fuss for such a place; she could understand Mared's comment about no one visiting anymore. Diane believed that there was to be more to it than this.

The Royal Palace was situated in the middle of the fields which were engulfed in a thick, eerie mist. Turrets still remained on the sides of the building where many walls were reduced to a decaying state.

So this is it? Diane thought.

Diane took pictures on her mobile phone as she walked through the Palace grounds. She looked up at the darkening skies, completely unaware of someone watching on in the distance.

After every three steps, Diane noticed, there were rusted metal hatches with handles barely attached. Ever the inquisitive, Diane crouched down and attempted to open a hatch. It didn't budge. She stood up.

"For keeping prisoners." A voice from behind her said.

Startled, Diane spun around to see an old tall figure, male, kindly with grey balding hair, slicked back. Down on one side of his face, Diane noticed, the man had a bad scar. The skin around the scar was drooping as if it was peeling from his face. She noticed the dog collar around his neck. She rolled her eyes.

"Not another one?" Diane moaned.

“I beg your pardon?” The man replied, and to Diane’s surprise in perfect English.

“Nothing, nothing.” Diane couldn’t keep her eyes from the man’s face.

The man introduced himself as Father Dovak. He offered a handshake which Diane accepted; she still couldn’t take her eyes from his face. Father Dovak noticed this.

“Don’t be alarmed, my child.” Said Father Dovak.

“I am sorry; I didn’t mean to be rude. I…” Diane looked on, embarrassed.

“It’s fine. Many look at this face. I have accepted it. In time it has healed.”

Indeed his wound had mended over time since his conflict with a certain Hans Reigns.

“Were… you attacked?” Asked Diane.

Father Dovak smiled to himself. “Yes, yes indeed I was.”

Father Dovak started to reminisce, his face serious. Diane looked sympathetic towards Father Dovak.

“I hope they caught whoever did it?” Diane said.

“No, no I am afraid they haven’t, my child.” Replied Father Dovak. “But rest assured he will pay the price.”

“He?” Diane inquired. She was intrigued to know more.

Diane listened with interest as Father Dovak told her about an 'assailant' who wore a hat and long overcoat. Father Dovak claimed him to be a danger and scourge to their society. All this struck a nerve with Diane recalling her very own encounter with Hans Reigns.

Father Dovak took in the Royal Palace ruin and breathed in the air. "It may not look like much, my child, however, the history is." Claimed Father Dovak.

Diane didn't answer as she aimed her mobile phone to take another photo. Father Dovak watched Diane with great interest. "You see the mist from the fields over there; they never clear, ever. There is a permanent reminder of battle."

"Battle?" Quizzed Diane.

Father Dovak smirked, knowing full well that Diane's knowledge was non-existent when it came to his country, and therefore he could get away with saying almost anything.

Diane trained her mobile phone towards the eerie mist that engulfed the fields beyond the Palace. She pressed the button on her phone to take her snapshot. However, it was not the picture she expected. Diane did indeed capture a shot of the strange mist, but the screen showed the mist moving, dancing, twirling and becoming darker and thicker. It was alive. Diane looked on, stunned and horrified. Through the mist, a decaying hand reached out, flesh rotten. Diane froze to the spot. The mist suddenly dissolved to a blood-red colour. Diane's hands shook as she frantically tried to switch off her mobile phone. Father Dovak smiled to himself, knowing full well the place to be haunted. His face became all serious when Diane looked over, and she was almost looking for an explanation of what she just witnessed on her phone.

"You look unwell, my child; everything alright?" Asked Father Dovak.

Diane didn't answer. She hated these very words: '*my child*'. It reminded her of an elderly babysitter that looked after her when she was eight. The babysitter would complete her sentences with the same words which sent shivers down her spine. Diane looked at her mobile phone before putting it away in a pocket.

***

Back at 'Duvi Init' in room three, Diane was busy on her laptop, tapping away at the keys, writing her experience in the form of a diary. She glanced up every so often at the corner area; the blood and guts, and indeed the trace of any spider were sure enough long gone, not to mention that the 'monster' was safe and sound, locked away in Mared's stored shed. Or so he said.

Diane stopped typing. She looked at her mobile phone that sat nearby; she reached out to retrieve it, then thought against it. Her visions at the Royal Palace was still very fresh in her mind. Diane was adamant that someone was having fun at her expense and to say she was 'freaked' out was an understatement. Instead of her phone, she grabbed a notepad that was nearby which revealed underneath the phone bill itemised and with a line of blue ink scored through several numbers.

Chapter Four

The howling wind made several bright burning torch lights flicker and dance on a cave wall. In the middle of the cave, a pan boiled on a small dark stove which emitted red heat glow. Hans Reigns sat down on an old, worn, crooked chair that creaked under his weight. Using a wooden spoon, Hans stirred the contents of the pan. Hans embraced the simple nomadic life. From day one, he believed it was to be his destiny. The cave was his home, and that suited him just fine. No one knew where it was, and he could come and go as he pleased. A thick sleeping bag, which was propped up by a wooden frame, sat in a corner. Hans began to eat a paste-like substance from the pan; beside his feet, sat a small pile of ancient books, but Hans was determined and focussed on writing his own chapter.

A loud crack of thunder shook the cave. This was too close for comfort for Hans' liking. He placed down the spoon, stood up and walked towards the cave's entrance, taking a sip from his silver hipflask as he did so. A flash of blue lightning illuminated the cave, giving a brief glimpse of ancient markings on the cave walls. Hans purposely stamped on an object on the ground; a small silver crossbow flipped into his hands. He stood at the cave's entrance, poised. Hans felt uneasy as he pulled a bolt from a jacket pocket and loaded his crossbow. Like a sixth sense, he was ready for something or someone.

The cave was situated in the outskirts of Gurikel, more specifically the mountainous region of *Gutamineer* which dominated the skyline behind the capital. This mountainous region was treacherous for many a man, but nevertheless, a cave over halfway up proved an excellent base for Hans.

Outside the cave, it rained heavily, which began to drench Hans as he scanned the area. A flash of blue forked lightning lit up the city of Gurikel, which was just over seven miles in the distance. Hans stood on a crumbling, uneven path verge, which ran down the mountainside. However, it was not even six-feet in width, and beyond that, there was a perilous near three hundred and fifty feet drop below down onto ragged rocks and heavy undergrowth. So it was no surprise that Hans was cautious. The combination of the whistling wind and driving rain distorted Hans's vision; he wiped his face with his arm and looked around, turning three hundred and sixty degrees; nothing. A dark cloaked figure suddenly appeared, floating in mid-air behind Hans. Fierce yellow, glowing eyes shone through the darkness and heavy rain. Instinct made Hans turn around; a squint of his eyes. He trained the crossbow on the dark floating figure.

A female voice whispered, spine-chilling. The figure gave an ominous warning to Hans. “I have come for you. I cannot fail roaming the Earth in this form.”

Hans recognised the familiar voice behind the black, floating robe.

“What has he done to you?” Asked Hans. “I have failed him. But never again.” The female voice cackled.

“Everyone will be a failure to him.” Hans shouted out above the whistling wind.

“He has cursed you to eternal damnation!”

“No, no, no. It is you that is cursed!” The voice laughed maniacally as it pointed a decaying finger at Hans.

Hans clutched his crossbow tightly, ready for battle as the figure floated high above Hans and from side to side almost toying with him. Hans aimed his crossbow upwards at the figure.

“Your weapon cannot hurt me!” Hissed the figure.

“Shall we find out?” Asked Hans.

Through the heavy rain, the figure twisted and turned like a kite through the air, yellow eyes still looking down on Hans.

The figure ascended higher into the darkness, out of sight. Hans shuffled around, crossbow at the ready, anticipating. The silence of the night was soon taken over with the sound of laughter and sinister cackling, pure evil. Hans couldn't see where it was coming from. The laughter became closer and closer and then silence.

"Come on, come on! Show yourself." Demanded Hans.

Hans shielded his face with his free left arm from the driving rain. From nowhere out through the rain and darkness, the decaying skull of Ina, the cafe owner screamed towards Hans as her headless torso floated peacefully in mid-air. Hans fired his crossbow; the bolt went harmlessly through the decaying skull.

Church bells rang out which heralded the break of dawn. Hans looked from his cave out to a beautiful sunrise over the city of Gurikel. His head was filled with images. He felt alive and curious. Suddenly his eyes shot open. What DID that dream or vision mean? He was both nervous and engaged by it. As he wiped the sweat from his brow, Hans thought about the battles that lay ahead.

***

Outside Ina's cafe, there was a hive of activity. A flurry of people, including forensic officers and police, went in and out of the cafe. Hans took a drink from his silver hipflask as he stood watching from a safe distance when a small-time journalist approached him.

"So tragic." Said the journalist.

"What is?" Replied Han.

Almost on cue, Hans watched a body being wheeled out of the cafe.

"The owner, found decapitated, head clean off." The journalist flicked through a few pages of his crumbled notebook, struggling to find what he was looking for; eventually, he stopped at a page. "Ina, is it?"

With these words, Hans became apprehensive. Questions began to run through his mind. Was the dream a premonition? Was Ina now to haunt him for the rest of his days?

The journalist called out as he watched Hans walk away. "Can you tell us anything about this?" Hans continued his walk down the street, ignoring the journalist. "I know who you are." The journalist called out.

Hans sat on a set of steps at the side of a busy market street, watching the world go by. Some traders barked out their selling pitch; others would literally jump in front of potential customers trying to sell them; clothing, food, junk and any other such items of worth. Hans shook his trademark silver hipflask, the contents of which were plenty. A small boy, not even seven-years-old dressed in rags, face blackened stood in front of Hans and gave him a sympathetic look. The boy produced an orange and offered it to Hans, who looked at the boy with his dark, sad eyes and smiled at him before declining his generosity.

A voice called out in the background; the boy dropped the orange in a panic as he ran back to his mother who shot Hans a harsh glance.

The sound of running water suddenly alerted Hans; he stood up, walked down the steps and looked up the street. He saw nothing out of the ordinary until he looked down at his feet to see blood flowing over his shoes. A small stream of blood ran down the street. Traders and civilians were perhaps oblivious to it because they continued to go about their businesses. Hans looked down at the dropped orange to see it unpeel before his very eyes, revealing a blood-covered heart which began to dissolve into the flowing blood. Hans looked up, beyond the traders and civilians to see a large dark, ominous figure.

"Zvekios!" exclaimed Hans. He reached into his overcoat and produced his crossbow. He ran fearlessly towards the dark, ominous figure through the flowing blood. Civilians screamed out in terror, seeing Hans, armed and charge up the street. He scarcely ran fifty yards before stopping to see water running from a burst pipe. The large figure, who he believed to be the Zvekios, was also gone. Hans, perspiring and gasping for breath, turned his head back down the street to see traders and civilians all looking at him, faces showing both anger and confusion. Hans immediately put the crossbow inside his coat.

A group of some civilians ran for shelter as a strong wind picked up, kicking up a small sandstorm which was enough for many traders to pack up for the day. Several stalls closed the shutters with a chorus of *thuds*. One trader, called Nikhits, wearing a red baseball cap at an end stall, completed his last transaction of the day. He reached out for the shutter when a man, with his face wrapped in rags, stood before him. Nikhits shielded the wind and sand from his eyes whilst he tried to get a look at the man, past the rags. The thick scarf entwined with yellow, blue and green colours, seemed to have been wrapped around the neck and face of the man forever. Nikhits made out a pair of beady eyes.

"The stone you have, how much?" Inquired the man.

Nikhits ignored the question, knowing very well what he meant. He made out he was busy as he began to pack small boxes and a suitcase into his clapped out small rusted car. “I have no stone.” claimed Nikhits.

Nikhits was hoping these simple words were enough for the man to disappear as the wind became stronger with each passing second.

The man shuffled around, impatient and clearly not accepting Nikhits’ answer.

“The one I saw you pack in your vehicle.” The man claimed.

Nikhits swallowed nervously. “Ah, that one.” Nikhits became immediately alarmed at the fact that he was clearly being watched.

“Yes, that one!” The man snarled.

Nikhits was uncomfortable with the situation by every passing second and shuffled closer to the driver’s door of his vehicle, planning to make a quick getaway.

“It’s not for sale.” Nikhits was firm in his tone as he finally got round to closing the shutter from his stall. “Now if you will excuse me.” Nikhits added.

The man came a few steps closer, which troubled Nikhits. “Then why bring it to your stall?” He said. Nikhits was done talking; he avoided the question as he opened the door to his car and squeezed himself in. He turned his head to the man.

“Good day to you.” Nikhits said as he ‘tipped’ his baseball cap to the man. Nikhits started up his car with urgency; he smiled satisfied as he began to drive away. However, the smile soon evaporated from Nikhits’ face seeing the man in the passenger seat next to him. He seemed to have appeared like magic.

A stunned Nikhits slammed on the brakes, which kicked up a large cloud of dust that engulfed the car. The man looked at Nikhits, deadly serious.

“I can’t let you leave with the gem.” His voice threatening. From a side trouser pocket, Nikhits whipped out a small blade and lunged at his unwanted passenger, but he stopped in mid-strike. Something had a hold of him; he was no longer in control of his body. Nikhits began to sweat in fear; he couldn’t move. He looked at the man, whose eyes were now glowing yellow.

The sand storm became more violent as the man emerged from the car. He held a blade in one hand; fresh blood dripped from the tip of it. In his other hand, he held the gem which emitted a bright emerald green glow.

Something metallic suddenly struck the back of Nikhits’ car just missing the man who looked at a hole at the back of the car. He turned his head to see the figure of Hans, his long coat flapping in the wind as he appeared through the swirling sand. The man jumped back into the car, the engine revved and wheels screeched, churning up dust clouds. Hans aimed his crossbow; he fired a couple of bolts at the car now speeding away into the distance. One bolt missed completely whilst the other shattered the back window but clearly had no effect as the car disappeared from the view. Hans threw his crossbow to the ground in frustration.

Chapter Five

It was mid-morning on a glorious October day. Diane stood waiting, outside the 'Duvi Init' next to a small table and two chairs with a folder under her arm. She was about to go inside when she heard a chair scrape on concrete. Diane turned to see a woman, wearing a pair of sunglasses, smoking a cigarette. "Nadia?" Asked Diane.

"You called me. You wanted to talk, so talk." Nadia dressed all in black was blunt and got straight to the point. Diane looked around before taking a seat across from Nadia.

"I never expected you to come," said Diane. Nadia, taking a draw on her cigarette, looked at Diane, who opened her folder and removed some papers. Nadia immediately stood up; something clearly had spooked her.

"What is it?" Inquired Diane. Nadia pointed at Diane's paperwork, strewn on the table. "I must go now." Said Nadia.

"I shouldn't be here. And neither should you!" Nadia said.

"Some questions are not meant to be asked." With that warning Nadia hurried away.

"Wait! Please!" As Diane followed, a breeze sent her paperwork scattering and swirling in all directions of the table. Diane chased and collated all her paperwork and put it back into her folder as quickly as she could before chasing Nadia again.

Nadia was well ahead; she had a quick glance over her shoulder, and she picked up the pace as she noticed that Diane was in pursuit. As Nadia crossed the road, she took a final look towards Diane before out of nowhere Nadia was struck by a speeding truck. Diane recoiled in horror, witnessing Nadia's body being hit so hard that it somersaulted in mid-air before landing on the metal pole of the market stall, which skewered her body. Diane turned a shade of pale. A hand was placed on her shoulder; she turned to see Mared. "Let's get inside." Said Mared as he placed a comforting hand around Diane, who looked across to see a small gathering already surrounding Nadia's body.

In the 'Duvi Init', Diane covered her mouth as she sat at a table in a small back room; the stench was back; back with a vengeance. The back room was practically a converted store cupboard and contained a small mantelpiece. Above the mantelpiece, hung a picture of the past Ubarian Royal Family. Mared placed a cup of coffee in front of her. Diane forced a smile.

“Thanks.” They both looked at each other. The two of them had plenty to say, but no one was willing to make the first move.

“You are in shock.” Claimed Mared.

“You don’t say!” Replied Diane as she took a sip from her cup. “How is the project going?” Mared asked. Diane responded with a forced smile.

“That good?” Quipped Mared. Diane put her head in her hands; the image of the impaled Nadia had engraved on her mind. Mared looked at Diane.

“Do you wish anything stronger; a drink I mean?” Asked Mared. Diane, without looking up, acknowledged Mared with a hand gesture, ‘no’. Mared took a seat across from Diane who looked across at him.

“Were you going to meet that woman, for your project?”

Diane looked up to the ceiling.

“Sorry, I talk too much.”

Diane got to her feet and walked out the door. Mared had passed the point of annoyance, and Diane had had enough.

***

Through the heavy driving rain, a hooded figure breathed heavily as they ran down the street as if their life depended on it. The figure ran down a set of steps towards a rusted metal door.

"Remember me?" The hooded figure turned to see Hans aiming his crossbow.

The figure, male, late thirties stood and smiled at Hans before his face 'morphed' into an evil demon face with yellow eyes. The demon had one final look at Hans before giving out a '*hiss*'. The demon levitated towards Hans, attacking at a fierce pace. Hans fired a bolt from his crossbow which struck the demon right between the eyes. The demon screeched and wriggled in agony before falling to the ground. Hans watched the demon as it dissolved into a green slime substance. Hans turned his attention to the rusted door; he began to kick the door repeatedly, which finally opened with a crash, giving out a thunderous echo.

Hans looked into the vacuum of darkness; he began to cough and spit, fighting against the smell. This whole city stunk, of evil and danger. From an outside pocket, he produced a small torch that he clipped on to the end of his crossbow. The torchlight illuminated a long passageway covered in cobwebs which resembled ghosts as they moved around in a chilly breeze. Hans followed the passageway with caution, aiming his crossbow in all directions. Laughter suddenly echoed throughout the passageway, followed by the shuffling of feet, which came from more than one being. Hans stopped at two tunnels, the one on the right being slightly smaller in size. Hans made his choice; he selected the larger tunnel on the left. He barely made a dozen steps when a pair of arms came bursting through the tunnel wall.

Hans scarcely had time to raise his crossbow. The very next second, a figure emerged through the wall, then a second possessed figure. Hans fired his crossbow repeatedly: one, two, three, four bolts, which took out the two figures. Hans always fired two bolts into his target; it was his policy just to make sure the job was finished. A third and fourth figure emerged from the tunnel.

"The Horde!" Stated Hans.

The 'Horde' was a group of possessed beings under the control of Father Dovak. They resided in the depths of the city of Gurikel and brought terror whenever Father Dovak desired. The 'Horde' came in all shapes and sizes, but all had the same cold, lifeless, unforgiving bluish-grey face with glowing yellow eyes.

Hans swung his crossbow aggressively against these creatures of darkness; the torchlight still clipped on the front of the crossbow shined like a spotlight as it moved in all directions. The crossbow connected with a sickening crack to the skull of one of the 'Horde' which barely stunned the creature. Hans went for another swing of the crossbow; the creature grabbed the crossbow mid-air but inadvertently activated a thin metal spike near two-feet in length which sprung out from the front of the crossbow and pierced through his eyeball making him *hiss* out in agony.

"Damn, I forgot about that!" Hans said with a wry smile as the 'Horde' slumped to the ground with a piercing scream. The remaining 'Horde' took a few retreating steps backwards.

"You like my modification, not bad; wouldn't you say?" Hans shined the torchlight directly into the eyes of the remaining creature who shielded his face. From an outside jacket pocket, Hans produced a small black sphere. He looked at it, tossed it up in the air and caught it. He smiled to himself.

"Want to play catch?" Asked Hans. He threw the sphere past the 'Horde' down the tunnel. The sphere discharged a smoky haze, a gas to be precise. "Time to say goodbye." Hans whispered.

From above, cracks appeared on the street and buildings began to shake, several passers-by stood looking at one another in both fear and bewilderment. Hans appeared covered in dust and cobwebs at the top of the stairs; he stood casually wiping his shoulders and bowed his head at the passers-by.

"My apologies. Last night's supper." Hans remarked.

Hans sat at a corner table in a side street bar; a glass of scotch and his hipflask sat on the table in front of him. Thoughts ran through his mind, namely hoping that it was the last 'Horde' he had seen. All was peaceful until a burst of loud laughter erupted from the bar area broke Hans from his thoughts. Hans took a sip of his scotch curiously looking at two large men, both suited, standing at the bar with their backs to him. Between the two men, Hans glimpsed a woman seated, wearing a pink hat getting agitated. Both men simultaneously rubbed the woman's back suggestively. Hans took another drink of his scotch, eyes not leaving the two men. The woman attempted to leave her seat, but one of the men pushed her aggressively back down on the seat. She wasn't going anywhere fast. Hans had seen enough; he slammed down his scotch and made for the bar area, face full of rage. As Hans approached the bar, the woman stood up, shrugging her unwanted suitors away. In doing so, she inadvertently knocked her hat off, revealing Diane. Hans stood astonished as the two would-be suitors skulked away in retreat past Hans. Diane picked up her hat, looking directly at Hans.

“This is becoming a habit.” Diane said as she put her hat back on and took her folder from the bar.

“I came across to see if all was alright; only I didn’t realise it was you.” Stated Hans.

“Well, as you can see, I handled this by myself.” Diane snapped.

“So I can see.” Replied Hans. “Now, if you will excuse me,” said Diane. She shot Hans a harsh look, and one of complete distrust.

Diane passed Hans without as much as a word. Hans noticed Diane’s folder. “How is the reporting coming along, Mrs Derry?” Diane stopped in her tracks, giving out a tiresome sigh.

“It’s coming on just fine. And it is *Miss* Derry!” Diane was becoming more irate in Hans’s company, and he just knew it.

“My apologies.” Hans said, attempting to defuse the situation slightly. Hans received a final look from Diane before she left the bar. He began to follow. A chorus of car horns being blasted nearby echoed throughout the area as Diane made her way up the side street. Hans swigged from his hipflask, keeping a slight distance as he watched on.

The afternoon air became colder in Gurikel; the sunset was not far away. Outside the ‘Duvi Init’, Mared crouched down whistling a happy tune as he finished painting the bottom of the front door, a light grey colour. He stood up and took a few steps back, inspecting his handy work, breaking a smile to himself. He was happy with his handy work. Mared suddenly winced and cried out as sharp pains shot across the side of his head. He placed a hand on his head. He looked down at the ground to see drops of blood.

What the hell: he thought as he touched his nose; blood flowed freely and ran between his fingers. The pain became more severe. Mared ran into the 'Duvi Init'; his hand reached for the telephone in the reception area, but he didn't make it. Mared slumped to the ground, the pain becoming more intense by the second until he passed out. Blood trickled from his nose and ear canal.

Literally, moments later, a shaken Diane entered the 'Duvi Init' to see Mared's unconscious body lying in an ever-increasing pool of blood. Diane swallowed; she took a few steps forward towards the reception area. Behind Diane, Hans Reigns stood in the doorway.

"There is no point in that." Hans called out. He walked into the 'Duvi Init'. Diane hung up the telephone. Hans locked the front door and pulled down a blind. Diane became uncomfortable. "You're stalking me now?"

Hans didn't answer the remark as he leaned over Mared's body and checked for a pulse. There was none.

"I am afraid Mared is dead." Diane looked around in disbelief. Fear suddenly came over her.

"You knew him?" She asked.

"Nearly everyone knew Mared. He was a lousy gambler. Always in over his head." Replied Hans.

"So how... how... did this happen?" Diane walked a few steps closer to Hans for answers and indeed, some form of comfort.

"Why don't you tell me, Miss Reporter?" Hans glowered at Diane.

"You don't think..." Diane couldn't complete the sentence as she gestured to Mared's body.

"Well, you were here before me," said Hans.

"By seconds." Diane replied.

"That is all it takes." Answered Hans.

Both Hans and Diane shuffled around the reception area, looking uncomfortable and for different reasons.

"Perhaps he got in over his head and owed people money, I did see..." Diane's explanation was suddenly cut short by Hans.

"Forces of darkness!" Claimed Hans.

"I beg your pardon?" Answered Diane, puzzled.

Hans began to pace around. “You are a long way from home, Mrs Derry.” He stated.

“Are you purposely doing that to annoy me?” Diane began to get agitated.

“What?” Inquired Hans.

Hans opened his mouth to reply when Mared’s head suddenly moved with a slight ‘twitch’. Diane noticed this too. Both Hans and Diane looked at each another.

“Uh, is that supposed to happen?” Inquired Diane, panting. Hans didn’t reply as he kept a close watch on Mared’s body. This time, the whole head turned to one side, which made Diane step back in fright. She thought someone was playing some kind of joke; however, it wasn’t funny.

Mared’s head ‘jerked’ left and then right. Diane looked at Hans for an explanation, one he couldn’t give her. A section of dark flesh emerged from Mared’s ear, followed by flowing blood. Something emerged from the ear, black and hairy. It moved. Diane jumped back in horror as her nemesis returned to haunt her. The spider or the ‘monster’ came out from Mared’s ear, ripping half the flesh off in the process. It was truly a horrific sight; one which made Diane vomit. Hans used his crossbow and fired two bolts into the ‘monster’ which obliterated it, sending legs and bits of body splattering in all directions.

To Hans, monsters came in all shapes and sizes. Diane's eyes rolled back, revealing the whites of her eyes before she passed out.

Chapter Six

While Dusk descended over Gurikel, Father Dovak sat on a granite throne inside an abandoned crypt under the deepest darkest depths of the city. Horns decorated each side of the throne. A hooded figure stood before him and presented him with the green gem. Father Dovak stood up, eyes wide open in excitement.

"Well, well. You are of some use after all." snarled Father Dovak. "Where did you retrieve it?" he asked. "Some junk stall in the outskirts, I had no problem with the dealer." replied the hooded figure. "Good work. You may leave." The hooded figure stood still in his spot, not moving an inch. Father Dovak was unimpressed, he declares, "Didn't you hear me?" Father Dovak. The hooded figure began pacing around uncomfortable and nervous. "There is something else." whispered the hooded figure.

Diane tossed and turned, her eyes flickered before she finally woke up. She looked around until the thing up caught her attention, Diane saw the beautiful sculpture of Angels playing trumpets. To her shock, Diane thought this was the afterlife. Diane sat up in a panic to take a closer look at the marble statue of Christ. Ultimately, Diane realised she was in 'The Zainitial'. She let out a sigh of relief and mumbled, *"The Grand One"*.

"You know your history." Father Nosro Sellew said as he took a seat beside her. "How are you feeling my child?" he enquired. Diane looked disorientated. "Is it dead?" she asked Father Sellew. The voice of Hans Reigns came from behind, "You are safe." Diane turned her head to Hans, who was walking down the aisle. "You can rest easy. I destroyed it.", said Hans while lifting his crossbow. Diane closed her eyes, satisfied with the revelation. Many thoughts raced through her mind as she looked at both Father Sellew and Hans, namely why she has been brought to the '*The Zainitial*'.

"You look confused" stated Hans. "Why did you bring me here?" asked Diane. "And tell me, why ever not my child?" Father Sellew said as he stood up. "This place is better than most. It is important to shield you from the forces of evil." "Okay?!" Diane smiled to herself as she watched Hans reload his crossbow with a couple of bolts. "So you fund Mr. Reigns here?" Diane directed the question to Father Sellew. Hans answers for him, "More like supplies me, we battle a common enemy." Diane began to laugh; she staggered to her feet. "This is nothing but a bad dream, right?"

Father Sellew watched Diane walk to the door, her high heels echoes as she exited. "Try and not let it become a nightmare, my child." Father Sellew said. Diane turned her head and fired back, "I am not your child! What is it with you guys?!" Hans casually took a swig from his hipflask and asked, *"You do remember the nightmare back at your accommodation?"*

Something suddenly dawned on Diane, "My laptop, my…" Hans interrupted her, "Under the front bench." he said. Diane walks to the front pew, crouches down, and looks underneath to check her belongings. She tries to slide them out from under the pew, but there was no travel case. Instead, it was replaced by a large white industrial-like bag which contained her belongings. Diane was irate, "What happened to my travel case?" Hans looked at Father Sellew, then at Diane "I broke the zip, apologies." Hans admitted. Father Sellew shrugged his shoulders; he didn't want to get involved. "Do you know how much that cost?" asked Diane. Neither Hans nor Father Sellew respond. Diane dusted off her possessions before inspecting them and prepared to leave with just her laptop. "Your project, how is it progressing?" enquired Hans. "For the zillionth time, it's progressing well." Diane shuffled around. Her body language gave a clear signal that her project was not progressing well. Diane walked towards the door and suddenly stopped, she turned to look at the statue of Christ. A thought came into her head. She faced Hans and questioned, "How would you like a job?" Hans looked at Father Sellew's perplexed expression. "Sorry, are you asking me?" Hans said. "Who else would it be?" Diane says sarcastically. "Isn't your friend there already in employment?" Father Sellew nodded his head in agreement comically gesturing towards Diane. "She is offering you a job." suggests Father Sellew. Hans eyed Diane sceptically.

"It all depends on the job." said Hans.

"I can pay you." replied Diane

"How much?" Hans fired back.

Diane walked forward in the direction of Hans and stands right in front of him. It's almost like a stand-off. "You will be paid enough, which would be paid in two installments." Father Sellew stood between Diane and Hans intrigued by the conversation. "So, you wish to employ Hans as a guide?" asked Father Sellew. "If that is what you want to call it, then yes." Diane replied. Father Sellew glanced at Hans, waiting in anticipation for an answer. "Why are you looking at me like that?" asked Hans. Father Sellew gestured with his hands in the air. "This has nothing to do with me." He skulked off to the other side of the Cathedral.

Hans looked at his crossbow, and then directly at Diane. He remembered the last time he was working;

deep down in the mining caves of Ramoor at the tender young and innocent age of eight. From dawn to dusk, six days a week for a period of three months. Legend has it that his father, The King of Ubaria, wished to set an example to his people by giving up his offspring to join the labour force at such an early age. Hans closed his eyes, recalling the *clickety-clack* sound the carriages made when they brought coal to the surface. The combined smells of sweat and coal with its damp, smoky stench overpowered young Hans to the point that he nearly passed out several times. It was only the good fortune of Hans that a fellow teenage worker whose name was never revealed provided for him. Hans never could repay the teenager who disappeared under mysterious circumstances soon afterward. He only recognized the teenager by a silver chain that he wore around his neck; it gave off a cascade of a rainbow light every time the rare event of sunlight hit it.

Father Sellew placed a hand on Hans's shoulder, breaking him from his thought.

"So, where should we start Miss Derry?" Hans asked.

Father Sellew was deep in thought; a past comment came back to him. "My child" He looked direct at Diane.
"What?" Diane snapped.

"You said and I quote, 'what is it with you guys?'"

said Father Sellew. "When?" asked Diane. "When you referred to my child." replied Father Sellew.

"I got that from another guy the other day out at the Palace." Diane replied.

Hans looked to Father Sellew, they both knew who Diane meant immediately. Diane noticed the strange look. "What? What did I say?" asked Diane.

Diane and Hans stood at the side of the street which was covered in a thin layer of grey dust. Crumbling tenements that looked like they were going to collapse at any minute occupied each side of the small street. Diane looked up and found a male occupant with a cigarette dangling from his mouth. He stared back down at them with interest.

"So, why are we here standing in the middle of a street like a couple of loony's?!" enquired Diane who minute by minute was getting rather annoyed.

"When do I get my first installment?" Hans asked.

"When will you tell me what we are doing here?!"

"That, over there is the reason for coming here."

Hans pointed at a gap in the tenements towards the *Gutamineer* mountains.

"Yeah, it's a very nice view, nice with snow on the tops, very pretty. So, what?" Diane asked.

"That is my home" Hans replied. "Isn't it beautiful?"

Diane looked at Hans unsure if he was having a laugh at her expense or being genuine.

One late afternoon Diane entered the cave carrying her laptop. She was greeted by flaming torches which illuminated the small dark stove and an old worn crooked chair. She noticed a sleeping bag propped up by a wooden frame that sat in the corner. Diane was astonished. Hans was deadly serious.

"You have to be kidding me!" remarked Diane. Hans stood behind her, clutching Diane's bagged-up belongings. Hans was proud of his home. *"You like it?"* Diane shook her head, "All that time and effort to get up here… for this?!" "Time and effort?!" Hans commented. "You didn't even walk a mile." "What do you mean walk? I would call that one hell of a hefty climb!" said Diane as she inspected the cave.

"Did you know the distance doesn't even amount to one mile from the ground? That is what I am saying." Hans replied, placing the bag in a corner.

Diane faced Hans. "So, where am I supposed to sit?"

"There's the chair over there, or on the bed?"

"Whoa, steady on, I don't think so!" Diane quipped.

Diane placed the laptop on top of the bed. "And don't go thinking I am staying here tonight."

"The thought never crossed my mind." Hans replied.

"What did cross my mind was what you said back at the Cathedral." Diane took her chance, closed her eyes as she sat down on the chair which *slowly* gave out a series of *creaks.* Diane looked down at the chair and wondered if it was going to hold together or collapse at any moment.

"What did I say? Remind me." Diane said.

Hans struck a match off the cave wall and lit another torch revealing more of the cave, this time the cave got Diane's full attention, especially ancient markings and diagrams.

"You mentioned someone else said my child". Hans paced around anxiously, half expecting Diane's answer.

"At the Palace? There was another man of the cloth." Diane stood up fearing the unstable piece of furniture she was sitting on. She watched Hans clean his crossbow with a cloth. "I know who that is" Hans claimed.

"Is that so?" Diane said as she inspected the markings on the cave. She ran her fingers through them and took out her mobile phone for a picture which gave of a flash that alerted Hans. "What was that?" he enquired. "It was just my phone." Diane replied.

A sudden noise diverted Diane's attention towards the cave entrance where she could see a deluge of rain falling heavily. "Perfect. Just perfect." Diane groaned.

"Don't be fooled by the collar and the cloth. That man

is a source of evil" Hans said paying no attention to the weather outside. He has experienced all weathers like hails, thunderstorms, hurricanes, and snow.

Diane's face was written with uncertainty, which Hans took onboard. He tossed the cloth to one side and inspected his crossbow.

"That man you saw was Father Dovak. If you wish to employ me as your guide, then you need to listen to me and my advice."

Diane faced Hans, serious. "Well, whoever he is, he wasn't very fond of you either." she said. "But, of course." Hans replied. "The person that caused him facial damage wore a hat and a long overcoat. You wouldn't know who that would be, would you?!"

Hans casually took a sip from his hipflask, screwed the top back on, and wiped his mouth. "This is where your project really starts Miss Derry. But I warn you. You may not like what you both see or hear."

"I am a reporter Mr. Reigns. I expect the unexpected." Diane said as she inspected Hans's home. "This is all very nice and all, but I've seen enough here. I wish to get back to the city, before dark." Diane walked to the cave entrance; the rain became more aggressive, small streams flowed down the mountain, and wind suddenly animated Diane's hair.

"Well, I am afraid that's not going to happen." Hans said.

"What, me not getting out of here, or getting back to the city by dark?"

"Getting back before dark."

"Well before it gets *pitch* black."

Hans shot Diane a blank look. "What? You didn't think I was staying here all night, did you?" chirped Diane. "Not for one moment." Hans replied. Diane glared towards the darkening sky. Lights flickered, dotted orange lights at a distance below.

"Good, you are my guide, which means you can get me back to the city." Diane continued, "That is what I am paying you for."

After a moment Hans grabbed Diane's belongings and laptop. "For which payment? I haven't received anything, might I remind you."

"You will get your money." Diane said. "Now, get me back down there, will you!?"

Hans walked to the edge of the pathway. He looked down; the rainwater flowed past him, it was like a small river now. Hans cocked his head to see the top of the mountain from where water ran down like a small waterfall off the edges. At the top of the mountain, thick, heavy, and dark clouds had formed. "Hmm, just as I suspected."

Diane looked out at Hans on the pathway. "What?" she asked. Hans walked back into the cave. "It's too precarious." he warned. He dropped Diane's belongings and laptop back down. "What do you mean, too precarious?" Diane enquired.

"Just as I said, it's too dangerous to travel down. The surface..." Hans didn't finish his sentence. "You are joking, right?" Diane was becoming angry.

"I never joke!"

Diane lowered her head and rubbed the back of her neck. She was now both tired and frustrated.

"You can leave if you so wish. However, I wouldn't recommend it. I put my neck on the line for many things Miss Derry, but stupidity is not one of them." Hans explained.

"Okay, I get it. You made your point!" Diane snapped. Her temper began to boil over.

Hans walked to the stove and almost like magic it produced a fiery warm red glow.

"I will sleep on the chair." Diane stated.

"Very well."

Diane opened her laptop case, took the laptop out, and switched it on. "Of all the places I've been working on a laptop. A first for everything I guess." The laptop emitted blue light from the screen. Diane glanced at the battery power icon at the bottom right corner. “Thirty-four percent, perfect.”

Hans moved blankets and cushions around his bed; he pushed out the creases on his cover with the palm of his hand. “We will get you plugged in tomorrow.” Hans said. Diane smiled for the first time in a while. “Don’t you mean charged?” she said.

“Is that what they call it?” Hans asked.

Diane smiled at Hans’s lack of technical knowledge. She didn’t respond, she didn’t have to. While Hans was busy on the stove, Diane watched him with interest. He placed the pan on the stove, and then, he opened a sachet, Hans pours the powdery contents into it and retrieved a bottle from under his chair. When he began to pour the liquid into the pan. Diane enquired. “What’s that?”

“Water.” Hans replied.

“Water? Where from?”

“Where do you think? Our very own mountains.” Hans added. “Pure as anything.”

Diane continued to watch as Hans stirred the contents of the pan until it became a thick, light grey paste. Hans picked up two small clay bowls and emptied the pan into one bowl. Diane didn’t like what she was witnessing and turned her head away in disgust.

"None for me, thanks." Diane said promptly. Hans looked at Diane, his face practically read like a board sign 'I am offended'. Diane quickly backtracked, attempting to rectify herself "I am just not hungry."

"Very well." Hans replied. "You don't know what you are missing."

"Oh, I think I do." Diane smiled, making light of her joke.

Chapter Seven

It was just after dawn and the sky was pure blue as far as the eye could see. However, there was a cold wind in the air. Diane stood on the edge of the mountain pathway and looked out onto the city of Gurikel almost in awe. The view was picturesque and attractive enough for Diane to take a few photos on her mobile phone. Diane was so wrapped up, she struggled to remember what day of the week it was let alone what date it was. She knew it was October that was it.

Something caught Diane's eye, it swooped and glided twenty-feet out in the sky. Diane watched this unusual bird, as big as an eagle. It was exotic with a brown body and streaks of green and blue. It landed on a ridge above, as the mountain tops in the background glistened like frosty crystals.

Hans appeared from behind and trained his eyes on what got Diane's attention. He found the bird fluttering its feathers on the ledge. Diane trained the mobile phone on the bird, ready for another photo snap.

"It's a *Wibherza*." Hans said.

Diane lowered her mobile phone. "A what?!"

"Legend has it that the *Wibherza* is a protector of not only the mountains but of the area." claimed Hans. Diane didn't acknowledge Hans. She found the claim totally absurd; she did however notice blood on Hans's right hand.

"Forgive me, did you sleep well?" Hans asked.

"I slept fine, thanks." Diane saw Hans with suspicion.

"Good."

"You've been busy." Diane looked towards Hans's bloodied hand.

"It was just a harmless accident." Hans stated.

"It doesn't look harmless. It could get infected." Diane warned.

"I have sterilised the wound." Hans said.

Diane eyed Hans sceptically as she walked back into the cave. "Can we get moving?"

"If you wish." replied Hans.

Hans took the lead as he carried Diane's belongings while Diane clung to her laptop case for dear life. As they both descended down the mountainside side by side, Diane took interest in the small dusting of bright red sand that covered the ground, mesmerised with the patterns being made by a gust of wind. Hans was literally yards ahead, turned his head to Diane who was crouched down with a hand on the red sand.

"That is what gives the mountain its glow. Like a beacon. Depending on the way the sun is shining, you can see it from a distance." Hans explained.

"So, I am effectively climbing up a desert mountain?"

"That is what makes it unique." claimed Hans as he looked down at the sand; which moved like the tides of the sea coming towards him. It stopped at his foot before morphing into a pattern, one of a devil's face. Hans quickly rubbed the sand with his foot and marched onwards.

Before Diane could say anything Hans thought it was an ideal opportunity to ask about Diane's career in reporting. He learned how she became a reporter from the tender age of twenty-one after college education. Diane reported on many stories but none stuck in the mind nor did they excite her aside from the robbery of a local store. The conversation soon diverted to parents, a topic that Hans had a habit of trying to avoid. Diane's parents divorced long ago, and several years ago her dad died in a traffic accident. She found it hard to shed any tears at the funeral, for which Diane feels guilty to this day.

"Everyone deals with grief differently. There is no right or wrong way." Hans suggested.

Their talk drifted back to Hans's family. "My parents are a distant 'flicker' in the memory." Diane stopped momentarily looked at Hans with a slight hint of empathy before continuing the relatively straightforward climb down the mountain. Later, she looked across at a heap of clothing wedged between two large boulder rocks. Diane thought nothing of it until she saw a foot sticking out from the clothing, she stopped in her tracks. Hans noticed something was amiss.

"Everything alright?" Hans enquired.

"I don't know. Why don't you ask that person over there?!" Diane pointed in the direction as Hans shuffled forward for a closer look.

"Your handy work perhaps?" Diane studied Hans as an air of suspicion grew stronger by the minute. "I mean, it does explain your bloody hand." she added.

"I told you it was a harmless accident. That over there was perhaps the job of the mountains' protector." Hans suggested.

"You mean the bird?" Diane carried on with her climb downwards, "I've heard it all now."

"Believe what you will. She would have swooped down purposely to inti…" Hans didn't get the chance to finish his explanation.

"On innocent climbers?" Diane wasn't falling for any fantasy stories.

"The people that climb this mountain are not innocent, or… all that they seem. They are guilty." Hans looked directly and in all seriousness into the eyes of Diane.

“Of what?” Diane enquired.

Hans didn’t answer the question as he looked up to see the *Wibherza* flying overhead. He watched it glide a good twenty to thirty feet lower, circling directly over their heads. Hans looked at Diane who stood shaking her head in disbelief.

“*That* is a protector and it can also read your mind?” Diane mocked as she pointed to the sky as she watched the *Wibherza* fly even lower. “I would like to have said that this was a pleasure Mr. Reigns.” Diane said. “Perhaps more of an experience I’d say.”

Diane shuffled a few steps forward when suddenly the ground beneath her gave way. Hans watched on in horror as he watched Diane disappeared from view giving out a piercing scream in the process. Hans dashed to the edge of the pathway, now with a gaping nearly six-foot-wide, he looked down to see Diane stuck on a shard of rock, only the strap of her laptop case is saving her from a precarious situation. If her laptop case strap were to snap, she would fall onto the rocks many feet below.

“Hang tight!” Hans called out.

“It’s not like I am going anywhere fast, is it?!” Diane proclaimed as she looked up at Hans, with her face bloodied and grazed.

Hans remained calm, masking Diane’s situation. He

rubbed his weary face and searched for something, anything at all that could be of some use. Her eyes were pleading for help, she was growing desperate by the minute. Beyond Hans, Diane saw the *Wibherza* circling overhead. She thought this was it, the prophet of doom from above sealed her fate. Hans got down on his knees in an attempt to reach out to Diane. She was simply too far away. To make matters worse, he noticed that the strap from the laptop case began to tear and fray.

"Grab my hand, reach out!" Hans said. Diane stretched an arm out as far as she possibly could; Hans laid down on his stomach on the ground for leverage wincing in pain as the sharp stones and debris dug through the clothing. Hans's fingers barely touched the tip of Diane's fingers. She was overcome with terror as the laptop case strap was beginning to give way.

The laptop slipped out and plunged down below, the case smashed into the rocks which sent the laptop into a million pieces. At the very last moment, Hans reached down and grabbed Diane's hand and laptop strap. With an almighty pull, Hans managed to get Diane onto the ledge albeit in an unconventional way that she scraped her face of rock whilst Hans fell onto his backside in the process. Both of them looked at one another, replaying the near-miss in their minds again as Diane got her breath back.

"Let's not do that again!" Hans said.

Diane touched her face in his disbelief and smiled. She suddenly began to see the funny side of her near miss. "How the hell can you live up here?" Diane looked up at the 'mythical' creature *Wibherza* soaring overhead. It was 'mythical' to Diane, she had seen nothing like it before. She was in awe of the creature as she witnessed it land on a ledge above.

"That thing must trust me!" Diane declared.

Diane looked over the ledge and saw the remains of her laptop down below. "That's my life's work down there." she said. "You still have your life." Hans replied.

It was early evening in *The Zainitial*, five candles were lit in different parts of the Cathedral. Father Sellew lit up the sixth and final candle with an old-fashioned 'spill'. He took a few steps away when an *eerie* breeze blew out the candles in one go which left the Cathedral with limited daylight. Father Sellew took a quick look around the Cathedral with a concerned expression. He gripped onto the crucifix around his neck.

Hans and Diane entered the Cathedral and Father Sellew practically jumped with fright. Realising who his visitors were, he looked to the heavens above, rolling his eyes and giving out a *sigh* of relief. As Hans and Diane approached Father Sellew, he noticed the wounds on her face.

"My goodness, what happened to you my child?" Hans took a sip from his hipflask before giving it a shake. It was almost empty.

"We were up the mountains as you call it." Diane answered.

Father Sellew shot Hans a look of disapproval.

"I think I should have included danger money for being a guide!" Hans burst into laughter. Father Sellew was stone-faced, he found the comment far from funny.

"Don't push it!" snapped Diane.

"Tell me, who was the one that saved your life?" Hans asked. Father Sellew gulped nervously, wondering where this conversation was leading.

On this occasion Hans had Diane there, she couldn't say anything to that.

"I don't think the venture up the mountains was a good idea." says Father Sellew.

"You're damn right they weren't!" Diane comments.

Hans paced around and put his hip flask away. He sensed something was wrong with Father Sellew, and wondered if he would be correct in thinking so, especially if looks were to go anything by.

"What?" Hans asked.

"You know *what*!" Father Sellew responded.

Diane felt uncomfortable with the tension between both men. "Am I missing something here?" Diane enquired.

Neither Hans nor Father Sellew acknowledged Diane's comment. Hans walked past Father Sellew, "I need to be topped up" he taped on his hipflask at the end of a pew and walked towards the statue of Christ.

"Shall we tell her?" said Hans. "What story shall we give Miss Derry?" Hans added. Father Sellew walked towards Hans.

"Why don't we tell her the one, where you can't leave this very Cathedral?!"

Father Sellew raised his arm in the air in anger and frustration. "Enough!"

"Perhaps I should leave you gentlemen to it." Diane said.

"Leave, yes. You and I have that luxury, whereas he can't!" Hans pointed at Father Sellew. He swipes away the hand in anger and grabs a hold of the hipflask. Hans unexpectedly begins to stagger around. Father Sellew closed his eyes, '*here we go again*' he thought. This has all happened before, too many times.

"Tell her about the curse placed upon you Father." Hans said, his behaviour slowly becoming erratic.

Father Sellew walked away with the hipflask, as Hans

slumped down. Diane approached Hans with an air of concern; she turned her head as she watched Father Sellew walk to the Cathedral's backside.

"What's wrong with him?" Diane called out towards Father Sellew.

"Take your pick!" replied Father Sellew.

"I heard that!" Hans replied.

"He will be fine. Give me a moment." Father Sellew called out.

Diane gave Hans a wry smile. Matters can't surely be that serious if jokes were being made she thought. She looked at Hans. "Honestly, cursed?" Diane shook her head, fed up with these 'fantasy' stories, and here was yet another one to add to the list.

Hans's right arm began to shake, he used his left hand to hold it still. There were both hot and cold sensations rushing over him, bringing him out in a sweat. Hans became weaker and pale.

An anxious Diane kept looking towards the back of the Cathedral hoping for Father Sellew to reappear any moment. Hans turned his head to one side, vomit splattered onto the concrete floor. Diane turned her head and closed her eyes in disgust. She covered her mouth. Diane called out. "Uh, you might want to hurry back there! He's been sick."

“I am fine.” Hans was adamant.

“You don’t look fine.” Diane commented.

Father Sellew marched down the aisle ways, his footsteps echoing the cathedral. His face was unsympathetic. “He can clean it up this time.”

“This time? This has happened before?” Diane remarked, looking directly at Hans.

“Never mind.” Hans replied.

Father Sellew handed a full hipflask to Hans who began drinking haplessly. Diane was stunned to see him drink as though he was stranded in a desert. The liquid ran down his mouth, past his chin, and dripped onto the floor.

Hans got to his feet and held his head. “He needs to see a Doctor.” Diane said with an air of sympathy.

“He will be fine, more to the pity.” Father Sellew growled as he gave Hans a ‘playful’ clip around the head as he walked by, Hans responded with a ‘*groan*’.

“What did you pour into the hipflask.” Diane asked, looking directly at Father Sellew. “My medicine.” Hans mumbled, head now in his hands.

“Clearly, you like your alcohol?” Diane said disappointedly. Father Sellew looked on with apprehension. “I don’t want a drunk as my guide.” Diane added.

Laughing, Hans got to his feet. “Did you hear that

Father? A drunk." Father Sellew rubbed his face and diverted any attention. Hans and Father Sellew had something to hide, a big secret perhaps, however, Diane wasn't going to know about it anytime soon.

"Mr. Reigns may be many things, but he is no drunkard." comments Father Sellew. Diane eyed Father Sellew sceptically, what are they hiding she thought. For the moment Diane gave them the benefit of the doubt. "Okay then. Show me what this country of yours has." Diane said, ready to seize the day.

Diane headed towards the main Cathedral door passing a small cluster of visitors. Father Sellew beamed a warm friendly smile as the visitors approached, who in turn shuffled by Hans who stood once again with his head in hand. Father Sellew watched the visitors move on to a safe distance when he vented his anger towards Hans, glaring angrily.

"What were you thinking?! Taking her to the mountains! You know what is up there." Father Sellew kept his voice down but it was loud enough. Hans gestured to him to keep it quiet.

Chapter Eight

Two backpackers, in their late teens or early twenties, male and female, surveyed the ruin of the Royal Palace. Bartok wanted to be anywhere but here as he wrestled with his large backpack. “So this is it?” he said, unenthusiastically, in a Scandinavian accent. He swung the heavy backpack over his shoulder. His girlfriend, Marthda, by comparison carried a small sized backpack and was too busy trying to figure out a local map to care or worry about Bartok’s tediousness. Marthda lowered the map and watched Bartok attempting to open one of the hatches just like Diane attempted, and also like Diane, it was of no avail.

“Careful, you don’t know what is under there.” Marthda warned. Bartok ignored her warning and heaved with all his might one final time. Nothing.

Marthda stood relived. “Some things are best left unopened.” She added.

Bartok spat at the ground, looked out towards the permanent fixture of the eerie mist.

“Do you believe all these rumours and myths?” Bartok asked. Marthda gave a feeble shrug of the shoulders. “Maybe they are consigned to the books.” Bartok said. “I will pick where we are going to next.

Can't be any worse than here, right?" Bartok added adamantly.

Marthda didn't answer. Instead, something caught her attention in amongst the mist. A small green glow shone through, almost alien like, and it was getting closer. Whatever it was, it had the attention of Bartok too.

"What is that? Over there, in the mist?!" Bartok asked.

Bartok thought it was an apparition until the tall figure of Father Dovak emerged from the mist like a phantom. Marthda and Bartok couldn't move, apprehended by the compelling figure of Father Dovak. In his hands, was the recently acquired green gem.

Marthda asked Bartok. "Who the hell is this guy?" Father Dovak was now just a few yards away.

"How should I know?" replied Bartok. "Maybe he's some kind of a guide?" he added.

Bartok was transfixed with the gem in Father Bartok's hand.

"Greetings." Father Dovak said, with a polite smile. Bartok and Marthda glanced at each other.

"How is your adventure?" Father Dovak enquired.

Father Dovak waited for an answer as Bartok and Marthda looked at him in confusion.

"You are backpacking, are you not?" asked Father

Dovak, gesturing to the backpacks attached over their shoulders. Marthda's attention was also drawn to the gem. Father Dovak smiled at Marthda and Bartok, who were focused on the gem.

"Beautiful, isn't it?" quipped Father Dovak.

"Now that would make a good stone for any engagement ring!" replied Marthda.

Father Dovak, laughed at the comment as Bartok was taken aback not knowing if Marthda was serious or not.

"Very good my child, very good." Father Dovak said nodding in the direction of Marthda. "What is your name child?" enquired Father Dovak. Bartok answered on her behalf. "It's Marthda." he said. "Martha, and what a lovely name that is." replied Father Dovak.

Bartok placed a protective arm around Marthda. "It's Marthda with a *d*." Bartok led Marthda away, he was becoming uneasy as Father Dovak watched their every move.

"Leaving so soon." Father Dovak asked.

"Well there's not much to see here, wouldn't you say?" Marthda replied.

"Let's say we've had a wasted trip." added Bartok.

Father Dovak's face turned both serious and sinister at the same time.

"And, why do you think that is my child?" Father

Dovak asked.

Bartok closed his eyes sensing trouble; he wanted to get out of here, fast, and with no explanations. Father Dovak was stalking potential prey. Bartok and Marthda took several steps when they got no further. They felt bricks were chained to their feet. Their legs suddenly became led weights and confusion turned into fear. Marthda glanced over her shoulder to find Father Dovak smiling. He was stalking prey, and now he could sense blood.

"I can't move my legs!" Bartok cried out.

"Me neither." Marthda replied.

Father Dovak asked with joy, "Problems?"

"I don't know what's happening?" Bartok panicked.

Father Dovak circles Bartok and Marthda. "Beautiful accents by the way, Scandinavian, yes? My my you certainly have come a long way. And contrary to what you have said earlier, this has not become a wasted time."

"Hey, what would you do if we were to take that stone from you?" Bartok asked. Marthda's reaction suggested otherwise. Father Davok who was enjoying every moment. "You may try boy, you may try."

"Please..." Marthda realised the situation they were in, but she refused to believe that they were up against the 'unnatural'.

Father Dovak aimed the gem towards Bartok, and something 'unnatural' started happening. Bartok was overwhelmed by fear, he looked down to as he sunk into the ground.

"Bartok!" Marthda screamed out of terror as her boyfriend slowly descended into the ground and she was helpless, incapable of doing anything. Bartok howled out in pain, he looked at his legs continued to slowly lower into the ground, as small streams of haze rose and swirled past him.

"Oh, I wouldn't worry too much my child. You will soon be in good company." Father Dovak said, pulling the green gem close him. "A little sacrifice goes a long way. This precious stone is just the beginning. The Zvekios needs this." Father Dovak added.

"Please… Stop!!" Marthda pleaded with tears rolling down her cheeks. Father Dovak smirked menacingly, ignoring her pleas. He was in charge of the situation. His eyes were wide with excitement as Bartok was now near waist-deep into the ground when his backpack detached itself from his body with an almighty tear. Marthda slowly slid along the ground unexplained towards Father Dovak. Marthda reached for Bartok desperately, but he couldn't even touch her. His hands were underground, and soon after, the arms were absorbed. Bartok succumbed to the 'unnatural' and hurled insults towards Father Dovak who placed his arm around Marthda. She stood motionless, frozen in shock and with tears flowing down her cheeks. Father Dovak wiped them away with his index finger, he owned her now. "I have plans for you my dear." Father Dovak smirked at Bartok. "She will be in good hands!" Father Dovak claimed before turning to Marthda. "Now for the best bit my child."

Marthda struggled to breathe, as she looked at Bartok for the last time. Three skeletons covered in dirt appeared behind Bartok, and with a chorus of synchronized roars dragged a screaming Bartok under the ground to his doom. Then, there was silence. All that was left was a small whiff of smoke, which twisted and danced in a breeze, the smoke morphed into Bartok's screaming face before it's blown away by the wind. Marthda lowered her head, the love of her life was gone. Forever.

"If it's any consolation, his flesh will be stripped first." Father Dovak stated.

It was mid-afternoon when Diane and Hans emerged from a ramshackle of a taxi, which is the usual kind of transport around these parts. Diane handed over the cash to the driver. The two stood in front of a vast woodland as the taxi pulled away behind them.

"What are we doing here?" Diane asks. "You haven't

brought me here to kill me, have you?!" she added.

Hans stood staring into the woodland, sensing his connection to this place. Hans took a few steps forward towards the woodland itself.

Hans finally responded. "Sometimes Miss Derry, you have to go back to where it all began."

"You're feeling better I see." Diane said.

"Never better." Hans replied.

"Talk about a miracle." Diane mocked.

Hans gave a slight grunt, disapproving of Diane's sarcastic tone. He marched towards the woodland. Diane took a deep breath and reluctantly followed Hans into the woodland.

"You referred to the beginning. Don't expect me to write your biography for you, if that's what you're thinking." Diane was adamant. Hans didn't respond to the comment.

"I doubt it would be a best seller anyway." Diane remarked.

The comment struck a nerve with Hans as he shot a look at Diane, deadly serious.

"Over time you would have enough information for many volumes of work, like the books I have up in the mountains." Hans said.

Hans continued his venture through the woodland.

Diane watched on, as he marched in front.

"I think you are bat shit crazy ol' man, and a drunk for that matter." says Diane.

Hans carried on his venture, knowing exactly where he wishes to be. He didn't even a glance back at Diane.

"I believe you turned to the church for solace and guidance." Diane called out. "Your stories are for the fantasy books." Diane added.

Hans shook his head in disbelief. "What about Mared? Is that fantasy? You don't know anything lady. Bat shit crazy? Ol' man? Huh?" Hans bellowed.

There were many thoughts scrambling through her mind as she looked around the woodland hoping for an answer to appear. Is this where you plan to kill me?!"

Hans burst out in laughter. "What? Kill my employer, before I have even been paid!"

Diane rolled her eyes. "Not this again." She mumbles.

"Besides, I would have killed you long before now, if I thought you were to be a threat." Hans claimed.

"A threat, little ol' me?" Diane jokes.

"Threats come in all shapes and sizes." Hans comment was all too real and brought back horrible memories for Diane. She shuddered at the memory of a 'monster' back at the Duvit Init.

Hans led Diane through the woodland, eventually

stopping a few yards before a section of heavy undergrowth.

"Why have we stopped?" Diane enquired.

"Over there." Hans pointed at the undergrowth.

Diane looked on bewildered. "What am I looking at?"

Hans walked to the undergrowth itself and pulled away branches and leaves which reveals a small rusted grid which was no more than six feet by six feet. This was the entrance to the coal mine from many years back, the one where Hans worked as a young boy.

"What you are looking at Miss Derry, is the beginning." Hans stated.

"I don't understand." Diane replied.

"I was a young boy when I went down there, to work."

"To work?"

"I used to work in the coal mines."

"What were your parents thinking?!" Diane asked, in an irate manner.

"It was my father that sent me down there." Hans looked towards the grid with sadness in his eyes. Thoughts, memories, and even the smells came rushing back to Hans. It was like he never left.

Diane stood silent, in disbelief. "Your father?"

Hans looked directly into Diane's eyes. "To prove a

point to his Kingdom." Hans proclaimed.

Diane's eyes widened, he had her attention now. She slid a hand into her pocket and pulled out a pen and a small notepad.

"He made his son work down the mines?" Diane asked, still in amazement. Hans noticed the pen and notepad in Diane's hand.

"I thought you didn't wish to write my biography." Hans gestures at the notepad.

"I don't." Diane fired back. "I am intrigued by this story, and what do you mean by 'his' Kingdom?"

Hans returned to his memories from all those years gone by, the flood gates were open and they came washing back in an instant.

Hans looked at Diane. "What do you think I mean, Miss Derry?"

Diane 'clicked' her pen repetitively, much to the annoyance of Hans.

"So, you have Royal blood in you?" said Diane with suspicion.

"No. It doesn't flow through me." Hans replied. "I was taken on."

"You were adopted?" Diane said.

Hans chose not to answer because he didn't like the word. He pointed towards the rusted grid. Diane stood in silence, the silence which is soon disturbed by the sound of her repeatedly 'clicking' the pen. Hans irritated, closed his eyes, "Do you mind not doing that please?" Diane sighed as she tucked the pen away.

"You don't believe me do you?" Hans asked.

"I've seen a lot of shit go on around here. But Royalty. You?" She scoffs.

"Why don't you ask Father Sellew?" Hans stated.

"He is almost as crazy as you?" Diane remarked.

"But he's a man of the cloth, and will always give you the truth." with that comment Hans's attention diverted to something else. He was swiftly alert sensing something wasn't right. He could hear the sound of snapping twigs amongst the undergrowth, and the sound came from somewhere nearby. Diane, completely oblivious, scanned the woodlands nervously.

Hans glimpsed an 'unusual' shadow moving through the undergrowth. Diane heard the heavy footsteps. She turned to Hans for an explanation but he was preoccupied. Diane could feel his vibe – all was not well, she swallowed nervously. Hans takes his crossbow out from under his jacket and yells, "Get down!"

A large and dark ominous figure sprang out from the undergrowth, drool dripped from ragged teeth, its fiery eyes glowed red. Diane cowered behind her fingers, as

Hans had his crossbow trained on the creature expecting it to attack. Instead, it took a firm stance and studied them. Hans observed the creature, a humanoid which moved on all fours, hissing and growling.

Diane lowered her fingers to take a glance at the humanoid creature in horror. She asks Hans who still had his crossbow aimed, "What are you waiting for?!" Hans stared into the soulless eyes of the creature; there was a connection that hit him but for the life of Hans he forgot what. The flash of a silver chain around the creature's neck immediately triggered him - the teenager who worked in the coal mine who disappeared under unexplained circumstances. Hans couldn't fire his crossbow. Diane wondered which of the two were going to make the first move. Hans pitied the creature, another victim of darkness. The creature hissed before scampering on all fours through the undergrowth. Diane watched as it pulled off the rusted grid and disappeared down into vacuum of darkness.

Hans lowered his crossbow and stood with his thoughts. Diane didn't know what to say or do. She did believe her eyes but what she couldn't believe was Hans's reluctance to use the crossbow.

"Are you going to tell me who or what that was?" Diane enquired. Hans rubbed his exhausted face. "I would if I could. But even I do not know.” Hans replied.

Diane began to circle Hans, confused. “I saw the way you looked at that ‘thing’, you know exactly who or what it is.” Hans walked towards the coalmine entrance shrouded in darkness. Something on the ground caught his attention, he crouched down to pick up the silver necklace that the ‘creature’ was wearing.

“That ‘being’ was someone who gave me strength when I went down the mine.” Hans proclaimed as he reminisced.

“So what happened, to him, I mean?” Diane asked.

“That I can’t explain.” Hans replied.

“How did he become... that thing we saw?” Diane said.

While Hans and Diane talked, they were unaware that from a distance they were being watched. The ‘creature’ again? No, the creature was long gone. The figure peering behind the trees was human and wrapped up, more or less like everyone else, in rags.

Chapter Nine

Hans was silent on the journey back to Gurikel. As they left the taxi, Diane attempted to lighten the situation. "Let's go for a drink." She suggests. Hans never took her offer. "Before you say no, I am buying." Diane added.

Something caught the interest of Hans from across the street, on a market stall; a lone woman wearing a crisp white apron with a floral design. The last time Hans saw an apron like that, he was helping his mother bake. He was six back then, and no one could've predicted the turn of events that would await them in the future.

Diane walked ahead, eyeing up an establishment. It looked quaint and exquisite, she thought to herself. Hans lagging behind her. Diane turned her head and waited for Hans to catch up.

"Well, this place looks as good as anything I have seen in a long time. And it has rooms!" Why didn't I see this place before?!" Diane said.

Diane attempted to take a few steps into the establishment when Hans stuck out an arm to stop her. Diane gave him a 'what the hell are you doing' look.

"Don't let appearances deceive you!" Hans quipped.

"What? Do the 'dead' rise at night in there or something?" Diane asked.

“They have known too at times. Yes.” Hans replied.

Christ sake. Diane mumbled as she turned her head away in disbelief.

"So where do you suggest then?" Diane inquired.

The place Hans had in mind was not too far away. He led Diane down to a steep cobbled street. This street didn't inspire Diane with confidence at all. From the top of the cobbled street, the same figure from the old coal mine watched Hans and Diane.

Hans approached the bar in question, where Diane stood, face totally unimpressed.

"You expect me to go in there?" Diane inquired.

Hans led the way and pushed the entrance door open. It was reminiscent of a cowboy entering a saloon with a mysterious aura around him. He swings the doors open, and the eyes move towards him. The stench of smoke coming from the combination of pipes and cigarettes lingered in the air. On this occasion, the prying eyes were sparse, half a dozen people at most. Hans gestured towards them with a nod of the head, and with that, the murmurs of chat resumed. Diane scanned the bar, where she was awestruck by the numerous pictures of the Royal Family that decorated the place.

“You won’t see me in any of these pictures if that’s what you’re thinking.” Hans commented. “I will get us a seat." Hans added.

"So, what can I get you? To drink I mean." Diane asked.

"A Dickentarum." Hans replied with a serious look on his face.

"A what?" Diane asked. She thought Hans was having a laugh at her expense. Hans smiled as he walked towards a corner table. Diane found a small coal fire in the corner, which made the place more homely. She smiled to herself. Maybe Hans had picked a not-so-bad-place after all. For the first time since she arrived, Diane felt at ease. She watched Hans at the corner table, taking a sip from his hipflask. Diane smiled to herself as she shook her head.

A woman, still in her teens, stood stony-faced behind the bar, staring at them without uttering a word or a smile. 'No greeting whatsoever. So this is how it's going to be', Diane thought to herself.

"Uh, just a Cola for me... you know a Coke, right?" Diane said.

The woman turned to a small refrigerator, the light of which flickered continuously. She got a tin of Cola and placed the can on the bar, *thud.* The woman took a random glass placed beside the till and placed it next to the can of Cola. Diane inspected the glass, which was grubby with greasy fingerprints. Diane's sigh of relief transitioned to a sigh of disgust within a matter of moments. Now came the main one.

"And uh... I don't know how to say this one, I hope it's genuine." Diane laughed to herself, making light of the situation, knowing what she's about to order. The teen was in no mood for any humour. She turned her head unimpressed as if to say, get on with it.

"You have a drink called a Dickentarum?" Diane inquired.

The teen knew what she meant straight away. She turned to the shelves, selected a brown bottle, and dropped something on the ground. The teen slapped down a photograph on the counter next to the Cola and the glass. The teen turned to pour the Dickentarum. Diane looked at the brown rum-like substance that was being poured in a shot glass. Diane looked at what the teen placed on the counter and thought nothing of the photo. Then, she did a double-take, her heart pounding. Diane picked up the old sepia shaded photograph and immediately recognised Nadia. But there was something else that made Diane's heart race.

Diane looked directly into the eyes of the teen. "Where did you get this?" she asked with a serious tone. The teen didn't respond. Diane didn't understand. Either the teen didn't want to understand, or she was just keeping quiet.

“Where was this taken?” Diane demanded.

No answer. The silence between the two lingered. Diane's patience wore thin. She slammed her hand on the counter, which alerted everyone, in particular, Hans. It got him out of his seat. Voices from the patrons piped up as Diane looked around. They glared at her unimpressed, with anger in their eyes. The tall and large male bar owner with grey hair aged in his fifties emerged from the side of the bar like a charging bull and let it rip with Diane. Hans attempted to calm the situation down, gesturing with his hands speaking with the owner in their native language. In the midst of the conversation and unseen by anyone, Diane slid the photo off the counter and tucked it into her pocket. The owner waved an arm at Hans, who ushered Diane away.

“What did he say?” Diane asked.

“You upset his daughter.” Hans replied.

Hans and Diane made their way out into the cobbled street. Hans sensed there was something. "What happened in there?" Hans said with an angry tone to his voice. "What made you lose your temper?" he added.

Diane walks with purpose ahead of Hans. Her walk soon breaks into a jog, albeit a feeble one. "Miss Derry…

Miss Derry." Hans calls out. Diane, ignoring his calls, reached the top of the road. "Diane!" He shouted. The first time he called her by her first name, and with that, she was gone, out of sight with a right turn at the top of the road.

Hans stood all alone while a small cluster of passersby looked his way curiously. Hans turned his head in their direction, and they disbursed in all directions like roaches scrambling away. Before Hans could move on, almost childlike *sniggering* is heard coming from behind him. Soon, the sniggering broke into maniacal laughter. Hans slid a hand inside his overcoat, held onto his crossbow, poised for action. Hans slowly turned around to be met by a dark-robed man, stooped over with a patch over his left eye. The man's laughter revealed missing and chipped teeth.

“You are too late.” The man exclaimed.

“For what?” Hans wondered.

The man began to laugh once again, taking pleasure in toying with Hans, the man enjoying every minute.

Hans abruptly aimed his crossbow at the man, who stood unfazed and continued to laugh. Hans gripped his crossbow tightly.

“What am I too late for?” Hans demanded an answer.

“Everything!” The man boomed.

At the main street, two small lizards ran out in front of Diane, who was now on her mobile phone. Diane stood watching the lizards chase one another. She flipped the photograph back and forth. On the back, in neat joint up black hand, the word 'Hanalbrek' is written.

Diane paced around, irate. She looked to the heavens hoping for an answer.

"You're telling me the next train outta here is not until Thursday? Well thanks for nothing." Diane snapped before hanging up on them.

A car appeared at a slow speed as it went past an unsuspecting Diane. The car came to a stop. Diane was oblivious and thought nothing of it as the car door creaked open. A figure came out of the car and approached Diane, who had lowered her mobile phone by this point. She frowned before backing away. The figure, like the man, was wrapped in rags.

Hans turned his head in all directions. He witnessed in the distance Diane speaking with the figure. Hans went in for a closer look. The rags that the figure wore flapped in the breeze, displaying colours and patterns. Then it struck Hans. This was the gentleman from the market, the one that escaped the bolts from his crossbow. He recognised the small clapped out small rusted car, the one acquired from Nikhits at the market. What Hans was unaware of, however, was the gem the man had in his possession that day, the significance of which he would be well aware of soon. For in high in his mountain home, he is the keeper of a similar gem.

The figure began to remove the rags wrapped around them. Diane stood, looking like she had seen a ghost at the man before her with a thick bushy beard, with tints of grey. His hair dark but greying, his eyes were tired with dark circles underneath, and two scars, one large and one small, were etched on his cheek.

"Yes, it is me Diane." The mysterious man said.

But this was no ordinary or mysterious man. This was Diane's long lost love, Jay Branson. The face she had as her screensaver on her laptop, the man she hasn't seen for nearly two years. And now here they are, in a strange country, thousands of miles away from home.

"My god." Diane murmured.

"You really found me. After all this time." " Jay said with a smile.

Diane stood motionless, with a tear in her eye running down her cheek. She was overwhelmed with shock.

"Get in. I will tell you everything." Jay suggested.

Seeing the events unfold from a safe distance, Hans watched Diane enter the car. Jay pulled away, making a u-turn, and driving in the opposite direction from Hans.

Everything fell into place. Hans's face dropped, and his suspicions were confirmed, noticing the hole on the boot of the car created by the bolt from his crossbow. All was now too late; Diane was gone, disappearing in the distance through a cloud of dust.

The sound of familiar sniggering that soon merged into a maniacal laugh was heard behind Hans. He closed his eyes, knowing who it was immediately. Hans produced his crossbow from under his coat and, without any form of warning or mercy, fired a bolt without even looking. It struck the dark-robed man, but he disintegrated into dust.

Something between the buildings caught his attention. Thick, dark smoke rose high into the blue sky. Hans's eyes widened, and his mouth was left wide open. He was shocked for the first time in a long time. He immediately recognised where the smoke was coming from.

Chapter Ten

Hans, perspiring, ran with determination on his face as he constantly glanced up to the sky, darkening and thickening with smoke. He leant on a railing, gasping. Hans, with old age perhaps creeping up on him, gasps for breath. He swallowed hard as he passed a small gathering; he was now in the clear as a horrific view of the Zainitial engulfed in flames, and smoke belched everywhere. Hans' thoughts immediately went towards Father Sellew, and his welfare summoned the energy he had left to sprint towards the burning Zainitial. Three men tried to prevent Hans from going anywhere near the burning flames, but he wasn't having any of it and shrugged off any advance.

Father Sellew emerged from the smoke and staggered around at the doorway. Hans rushed to his aid as Father Sellew collapsed to the ground.

“Get back!” Hans screamed at the gathering crowd.

Hans cradled Father Sellew's face blackened with smoke and bleeding with wounded cuts, deep and nasty.

“I... I couldn’t stop them.” Father Sellew murmured, wheezing.

Father Sellew smiled to himself, what a twisted irony he thought.

"The forces of darkness placed a curse upon me that I

could never leave this building." Father Sellew coughed and spluttered. His chest crackled with every breath.

“And now, they set fire to the place and gave me no choice.” Father Sellew added.

Tears welled up in Hans's eyes.

“No tears my friend, no tears. There isn’t time for that.” Father Sellew said. “You must stop them. End what has begun.” He continued.

“Not without your help.” Hans bargained.

Father Sellew forced a smirk. “It’s too late for that dear friend.”

Hans looked up at the blue sky being blocked out by the dark smoke.

“He won’t give you the answers.” Father Sellew said. “The only person you believe in is yourself.” Father Sellew claimed.

Father Sellew slowly reached out and touched Hans's battle-worn face.

“Where is the girl?” Father Sellew questioned, every word followed with a wheeze.

Hans closed his burning eyes. He wouldn't dare lie to a dying man, especially a mentor and a friend of many years.

“I can’t say. She went away with someone. A man I recognised from a market stall.” Hans replied plainly.

“No!” Father Sellew cried out, with his coughing and spluttering becoming more severe.

Suddenly, the Zainitial roof caved in with an almighty thunderous crash. Hans turned his head to see the marble statue of Christ smashed through the side of the ancient building broken into two.

"Find the girl, she could be the key to all... this," Father Sellew whispered. "Prevent eternal darkness."

Father Sellew reached out. His fingertips caressed his face for one final time. Wheezing continuously, Father Sellew gave Hans one last faint smile. With one final breath, his head dropped sideways. The wheezing grew until it stopped, forever.

Father Sellew's dead body began to decay before his very eyes until it turned into a skeletal state. This was a result of the curse placed upon him. The skeleton shortly turned to mere dust. Hans wanted to stay put, but he had to get up and leave, for there was no time for sorrow. There was much work to be done.

www.ingramcontent.com/pod-product-compliance
Ingram Content Group UK Ltd.
Pitfield, Milton Keynes, MK11 3LW, UK
UKHW020422250726
13967UKWH00007B/2777